For all the children of
Plan International
– *M.P.*

For Marian and John
– *G.R.*

Published in 1995 by Magi Publications
55 Crowland Avenue, Hayes, Middlesex UB3 4JP

Text © 1995 by Maggie Pearson
Illustrations © 1995 by Gavin Rowe

The right of Maggie Pearson to be identified as the author
of this work has been asserted by her in accordance with
The Copyright, Designs and Patents Act 1988.

Printed and bound in Italy by Grafiche AZ, Verona

ISBN 1 85430 273 6 (Hardback)
ISBN 1 85430 130 6 (Paperback)

Room for One More

by MAGGIE PEARSON

illustrated by GAVIN ROWE

MAGI PUBLICATIONS

London

It was a winter's night, starlit and frost-bright,
the coldest night of the year.

The travellers at the inn, though, were snug and warm.

So many travellers, making work enough for six.

But there was only one of Jenny, and a little one at that.

"Clear those dishes, Jenny!"

"Pour the wine!"

"Fetch water from the well!"

"There's no wood for the fire,
Jenny. Go out and get some more!"

Off went Jenny, leading the donkey to carry the wood, wrapping an old blanket round her against the cold.

Back they came again, the donkey nothing but a pile of wood on legs. There was not much to be seen of Jenny, either, under the blanket, but her little bare feet, blue with cold.

The donkey's stable was no more than a bit
of tattered thatch, leaning up against the wall,
with just room inside for one. But somehow
they made room enough for one more,
so Jenny could warm herself against the
donkey's coat before she went back to work.

In the yard a poor old ox stood all alone in the cold.

"Come into the stable," said Jenny. "There's room enough for another one."

And so there was – room for the donkey and the ox, too.

Back went Jenny to the kitchen, to serving at table and washing the dishes, and sweeping the floors, and tending the fires.

And here were two more weary travellers, a man and a lady.

"No room!" the landlord said to them.
"There's no more room at the inn!"

No room?

"Come with me," whispered Jenny when the
landlord had gone. "Come into the stable. We can
make more room there."

And so they did.

So now there was room enough for the donkey
and the ox and the man and the lady, too.

Upstairs in the inn the travellers were sleeping, four, five, six to a bed.

Downstairs they dozed on benches and tables, and draped themselves over the banister-rail.

Jenny went back to work till everything was spick
and span. Then, though she was ready to fall asleep right
there where she stood, she fetched bread and wine and
a few small fried fishes, and took them over to the stable.

"Come in, Jenny!"

"There's no room!" she said.

"There's room for a little one."

And there was – room for the donkey and the ox,

the man and the lady and room for Jenny, too.

And there was room for one more . . .

. . . a new-born baby, lying in the manger.

Jenny knelt down and gave the baby her finger
to hold.

She didn't feel cold or tired any more. She felt like
dancing.

Through the tattered thatch Jenny could see a
shining light over the hills.

The frost sparkled, and the tired old world looked
young again.

Somewhere out in the cold night there was music and
singing —

He has come!

He is here!

Christ is born!

Over field and furrow the message ran, waking the rabbits in their burrows and the sheep high up in the hills.

The shepherds heard it and came hurrying down.
A small shepherd-boy came too, carrying his pet lamb.

Out of the night they came to see the baby, the travellers woken from their beds, the shepherds from the hillside and others.

Where did they all come from?

"May we come in?"

"Is there room for us?"

"And me!" cried the shepherd-boy. "Is there room for a little one?"

And there was room – room for *everyone*.